ROBIN HOOD

WHO SHOT THE SHERIFF?

Adapted by Jacqueline Rayner from the television
script "Who Shot The Sheriff?" by Dominic
Minghella for the television series Robin Hood
created by Dominic Minghella and Foz Allan
for Tiger Aspect as shown on BBC One.

CHAPTER ONE

Life had never been easy for the peasant folk of England, but they had made the best of it. Good king Richard was on the throne and his subjects worked hard, practising their trades, taking their goods to market, earning the money to feed their families. Wise and just men, like Edward, Sheriff of Nottingham, had authority over them, and if taxes and punishments for wrongdoing had to be endured, at least the people knew they were fair.

Once upon a time. But now everything had changed.

Life was still not easy, but now it was also harsh and cruel. King Richard was away fighting in the Holy Land, and his brother John ruled in his stead. John's men now held authority throughout the country – and John and his men were neither fair nor just. A man might lose his hand for poaching, or his life for a theft. Taxes were raised to a level that few could meet. And a visit from the tax collector, once tolerated if not welcomed, was now an occasion for fear.

Owen the miller was feeling such fear. He had worked hard, as hard as he could, but he had been unable to earn the money that Vaizey, the new Sheriff of Nottingham, demanded. His debts had mounted, and now the bailiff, Joderic, was on his way to evict Owen, his wife Kate, and their children, from the mill that was both their home and their only source of income. How they would live from now on, he just did not know.

Owen did not really blame Joderic, who was a kind man, despite his disagreeable job. He knew that Joderic was under orders from the Sheriff. Owen had recently had to send his twelve-year-old son, Matthew, to work at Nottingham Castle to make ends meet, and so he was well aware that getting on the wrong side of the Sheriff was a dangerous, if not fatal, thing to do.

And so he was worried rather than reassured when Robin Hood turned up on his doorstep and informed him that everything would be made right.

Robin of Locksley, Earl of Huntingdon, had recently arrived back in England after fighting

3

alongside King Richard in the Holy Land. The stories had it that he did not like what he saw on his return and had openly challenged Sheriff Vaizey, making such a nuisance of himself that he was eventually forced to go on the run to save his own life. No longer able to watch over the people of Locksley officially, Robin had nevertheless set himself up as their saviour, and Owen wasn't the first to receive a visit from the noble outlaw. Now, Robin was trying to persuade the miller that he would, somehow, prevent the eviction.

'But how?' Owen asked him. 'Joderic will be under orders.'

'"How" is not for you to worry about,' Robin replied.

Well, that was all very well for Robin to say. Owen was only too conscious that just talking to the one-time Earl like this was risky. If it became known that he was accepting favours, perhaps even money, from him... He tried to explain it to Robin. 'I cannot be seen to take from you. I cannot even be seen with you.' He gestured at the boy standing a little distance away, by his sobbing mother. 'Our Matthew has to work at the castle.'

He could see by Robin's eyes that he understood.

But there was determination in those eyes too; Robin was not to be swayed from his course. 'Owen,' he said, firm but reassuring. 'Take your wife and family, and get your belongings back into the mill. Joderic will not evict you today.'

And suddenly Owen believed him, believed that everything would be all right, somehow. He could trust this man. They were saved. He had a fleeting desire to fold Robin into an embrace – but Owen was not by nature a demonstrative man. He contented himself with a nod. But the nod said a lot. Robin nodded back, and they understood each other.

Still half-disbelieving, Owen left Robin and walked over to Kate and the children. Smiling for the first time in days, he explained to them what Robin had told him, and had the pleasure of seeing his wife smile too, scarcely able to accept what he was saying. They were to keep their home! And all because of Robin...

Much was getting used to this, to the way the peasants reacted to Robin. And it was always Robin who got the adulation, oh yes, despite the frankly enormous and indispensable role that

Much played in all his master's schemes. Not that Robin was his master now, not officially – Much had been granted his freedom for those five long years of service in the Holy Land. But his devotion went so deep that words like 'servant' or 'free man' made no matter. Still, it didn't stop him regretting the course of action Robin had chosen, the way of life that condemned Much to a wild and hungry existence in Sherwood Forest instead of the relative luxury and full larder of the lodge at Bonchurch which he'd been promised...

And now Robin was just standing there, looking over at the miller and his family with a kind of expectant expression, though they'd done all they'd come for. If they had to carry out these mad benevolent schemes, couldn't they at least just get on with it?

'Let's go,' Much said. Robin seemed not to hear him. Much tried again. 'What are you waiting for?'

'Nothing,' Robin said, but still didn't move. A vaguely sheepish look flitted across his face as he continued to watch Owen and Kate and the children, and Much suddenly realised what it was. He raised his eyebrows.

'Oh, please.'

'What?' said Robin innocently.

'You want to see the look on her face, don't you? You want to see the gratitude.'

Robin, caught out, grinned guiltily. Finally he turned away and the exasperated Much followed him, on their way at last to do what they'd set out to do – deal with the bailiff.

Another thing Much was getting used to since his return to Nottinghamshire was hiding in bushes. It didn't seem to him to be a particularly desirable occupation for a free man, but he had little choice in the matter. If they were not hiding from the Sheriff's men, they were taking part in one of Robin's schemes, like now.

At the moment, Robin was somewhere to his left, and skulking in the undergrowth nearby were two of the others with whom they'd teamed up: cheerfully crooked Allan A Dale and gruff desperado Roy. They were all watching the path along which Joderic must come to reach Nettlestone village and the miller's home.

Finally there came the cracking of twigs and rustle of leaves that told of someone approaching.

Several someones, in fact. That made Much nervous, but as they came into view he saw, to his relief, that it was just Joderic with a couple of junior clerks in tow. Nothing to worry about.

As soon as Joderic drew level, Robin jumped out of the bushes to greet him. The tax collector was only momentarily taken aback. Obviously he had heard about Robin's return – and the developments that had occurred since then. 'Robin...' he said in recognition. In the old days – the good old days, as Much thought of them – they'd been well acquainted.

Robin led the old man to one side, out of earshot of his clerks, but still in clear view for the hidden Much. Joderic did not look happy that he had been waylaid.

'Do not interfere,' he said firmly, fixing Robin with a regretful but determined look. 'You know I have to do this.' He paused, and gestured to the path he'd just come along. 'And you know there are Sheriff's men on their way to make sure there's no trouble.' Much hastily glanced in that direction, but as yet the way was clear.

'*Do* you have to do this?' Robin asked, just as determined as the bailiff.

Joderic nodded. 'I did it under the old Sheriff. You did not complain.'

That was different, thought Much, and was surprised to hear his words echoed by Robin. 'That was different.'

'How?' Joderic asked. Well, Much could have told him. As if anyone couldn't see the difference between this new Sheriff, eager to bring the poor to greater poverty, and good Sheriff Edward. A wise old man, Much had always thought. In fact, Edward had advised Robin against this outlaw course, told him to work within the system to make things better. Very wise, he was. If only Robin had listened to him...

'Two things are certain in life: death and taxes,' continued Joderic.

Robin shrugged. 'But when the death is *caused* by the taxes, something is rotten.'

Much felt almost sorry for Joderic. It was clear that the bailiff did not wholly disagree with Robin, despite his official position. But he had a job to do.

Robin held out a large purse, chinking with coins. 'Take this. The miller's debts.'

But Joderic shook his head. 'I cannot. That is

stolen money. And the Sheriff knows the miller cannot pay – how would I explain it?'

A good point, thought Much. Robin was full of good intentions, but did he think his plans through? Of course the Sheriff would realise where the money came from, and what good would it do Owen and his family then?

But Robin was giving the bailiff that cheeky, you-can-do-it grin that had people falling over themselves to please him – as Much knew only too well. Who could resist?

Not Joderic, it seemed. His hand reached out, almost by its own accord, and accepted the purse, weighing up its contents. 'I could break it into small amounts. Pay it in over a period of time. That would be credible.'

The secretly watching Much nodded happily. Of course, he hadn't doubted that Robin's plan would succeed. Not for a second.

Robin's smile lit up his whole face. 'Every time somebody breaks bread in Nettlestone, they will thank you, Joderic.'

Joderic half-smiled against his will. 'Sure.'

And they'll be thanking you too, Robin, Much thought. The great Robin Hood, saviour of millers and other peasants. You'll like that. Not that he was saying that Robin was vain...

Robin had begun to turn away, but stopped. He'd thought of something else. 'Do me a favour,' he said to Joderic, 'tell them this is your own scheme. Tell them you have not seen me.'

'Why?' asked Joderic.

Robin grinned. 'My friends think I am vain!'

In the bushes, Much shook his head in disbelief. What sort of friends could they be? Certainly such an idea had never entered Much's head!

A warning call came from the trees behind: Allan. The Sheriff's men were on their way. Robin hastily stepped away from Joderic, melting back into the foliage at the side of the path until he was beside Much again and hidden from view. Together they watched as the bailiff slipped the heavy purse inside his cloak, and carried on his way through the forest as if nothing out of the ordinary had happened. Then, as stealthily as they could, they began to follow him.

CHAPTER TWO

As he rode on towards Nettlestone, Joderic wondered if he had done the right thing. After all, the law was the law, and he had been a servant of the law all his life; it was not for him to decide which were the good laws and which the bad. But as he tried to tell himself this he couldn't help but think of the things that had happened under the new Sheriff's new laws – things that had happened to people he'd known all his life, people he'd counted as friends. Owen and Kate, for example – they must have been in dire straits indeed to get so behind on their payments. Was it really fair to punish them further for their misfortune? No, he decided. It was right to have mercy.

Right, but not necessarily safe. He was taking a big risk. Robin had asked him to leave his name out of it, and to be sure he would do that. It would suit him fine not to have any connection known with the outlaw Robin Hood, much as he may have respected the young man when he was Earl of Huntingdon.

Nettlestone village came into view. Joderic spotted Kate clinging to her husband outside the mill, and as he got closer the panic in her eyes was plain to see. He regretted having to leave it there for a little longer, but he had to make this look realistic.

'Wait here,' he told the Sheriff's men, not wanting them to be able to eavesdrop on his conversation with Owen and Kate. Joderic rode his horse forward a few more paces then dismounted, walking towards the unhappy couple. Owen straightened himself up as Joderic approached, but an air of desperation surrounded him.

The bailiff raised his voice – this part the Sheriff's men could hear. 'Owen, Kate,' he said formally, letting no trace of a smile show, 'as you know, I am here today – '

But Owen interrupted, urgently. 'Robin – didn't you see Robin Hood?'

Joderic hesitated. He had to be careful now. Had to try to explain the plan to Owen, without revealing whose idea it was in the first place. Had to make it look realistic to the Sheriff's men; look

15

as if Owen had paid him a little money now to escape the eviction. So Owen had to keep calm or the men might get suspicious...

Joderic chose his words carefully. 'No – no, sorry, I have not seen Robin Hood – but we can work this out...'

Owen might have felt more reassured had he known that Robin and his men were hidden nearby, watching everything that was going on.

But he didn't know.

All he could think was that Robin had let them down terribly. That he'd been a fool to trust him, him and his brave words – words that had seemed so reassuring, but were now proved to be glib and false. After all, why would a noble – albeit an outlawed one – care about poor folk like them? No, Robin had let them down. Apparently he had not even tried to speak to the bailiff! But here was Joderic saying they could work this out...

And suddenly an arrow slammed into the bailiff's back.

Kate screamed.

Owen grabbed hold of her arm, and stared in disbelief as Joderic fell at his feet. Dead.

'He's killed him,' he said, suddenly realising with horror what Robin had meant when he said that Joderic would not evict them today. 'Robin's killed him!'

It took Robin and his men barely a split second to take in what had happened to Joderic, and then they were spinning around, looking frantically behind them for the shooter of the fatal arrow.

There, hiding in the bushes behind them, was a figure robed from head to toe in black, a bow in his hand and a staff strapped to his back.

Robin got to him first, diving forward confidently. But to his amazement the concealed figure was even quicker; the man's leg flew out and before Robin knew what was happening he was on the floor, gasping for breath. He could only watch as the man ran off into the forest, the other outlaws close on his heels.

Robin pulled himself to his feet, still winded, and staggered into the forest to join the chase. It wasn't hard to follow; the men were crashing through the undergrowth, speed more important than stealth. Finally, still breathing heavily, he burst into a clearing – only to find the outlaws standing there, gazing around themselves, chase abandoned. He only had to look at their faces to know the unwelcome truth – they'd lost the man.

Robin was furious. He glowered at his men as they carried on through Sherwood Forest. Will Scarlett tried to show something he'd made, a tag of identification, one for each of the outlaws – Will, son of Locksley's carpenter, was a natural craftsman – but the angry Robin brushed him aside. 'Not now, Will.'

Roy, who as a long-time outlaw and resident of the forest had less reverence for Robin than some of the others, challenged his foul temper. 'What's the matter? You can't believe somebody's better than you? He kicked you good.'

'Who is he?' Robin asked.

It was Will who answered. 'He's the Nightwatchman.'

'I have never heard of him,' Robin said.

'The Nightwatchman? Been around for years. Maybe you were off on the crusade,' Will suggested. 'He's a good man. They talk about him in all the villages. He's been seen in Nottingham. Even at the castle. Always at night.'

Roy joined in the explanations. 'Brings medicine

18

and stuff. Food. Sheriff's men have been told to shoot on sight. But he's never hurt a fly.'

Tell that to Joderic, thought Robin, remembering the last gasp of the kind bailiff as he fell to the floor. 'Sounds like he's decided on a change of direction.'

Sometime later, the members of the Council of Nobles took their seats in Nottingham Castle. Once upon a time, Robin would have been one of their number. But now his estates were in the hands of Guy of Gisborne, a dark-haired, dark-eyed man who strode into the Castle's great hall alongside the Sheriff of Nottingham.

The old Sheriff, Edward, was also present by virtue of his place on the council. With him was his beautiful daughter, Marian. At the moment, father and daughter were both dressed in mourning clothes, their faces showing sorrow at the death of a good man. By contrast, the Sheriff looked positively happy as he stood to address the nobles.

'My friends. Villagers in Nettlestone report that Robin Hood killed an innocent bailiff today – Jonathan.'

'Joderic,' Marian corrected him, determined that

19

the old man would at least be granted the dignity of his own name.

The Sheriff continued, still happy. 'Indeed, it is marvellous, isn't it? Such drama. What Robin Hood forgets is that even his beloved villagers have limited patience for heroes who pick them off.' He looked around the room. 'What else are they saying?'

It was Guy of Gisborne who answered him. 'Only that Hood was fulfilling his promise to prevent an eviction.'

The Sheriff raised an eyebrow. 'Well, war has addled his brain.' He addressed Gisborne directly. 'What would your response be?'

Gisborne didn't hesitate. 'Immediate reprisals against villages.'

Most of the council members seemed to accept this, but Marian leapt to her feet in protest. Gisborne stared at the girl in astonishment and fury as she shot his plan down in flames. 'Joderic would not want that,' she declared passionately. 'Why should more innocent people suffer because of his death? The same people who witnessed and reported this crime? And did this strategy of reprisals in the villages work before? No.'

There were nervous looks from some of the nobles: it was dangerous to speak out like this. Others looked patronisingly at the girl, anticipating the Sheriff's sharp response.

But the Sheriff just stood there for a moment, examining a scar on his hand. What no one present but himself knew was that Robin Hood had put the scar there – so he knew just how dangerous the outlaw could be.

'Marian is right,' he said. 'We're not going down that road again.' He turned to a nearby man who'd been paying close attention to the discussion: Robert De Fourtnoy, his Master at Arms. 'De Fourtnoy. Alternatives?'

'There… is a political advantage to be gained here,' De Fourtnoy began.

'Robin Hood has given us the high ground. We should keep it.' The Sheriff completed the idea. 'My thoughts exactly.'

De Fourtnoy hurried to expand on the new plan. 'We could have the town criers announce what has taken place. Make sure everyone knows he has killed an innocent.'

The Sheriff nodded. 'Good. We're going to win hearts and minds, gentlemen.'

With that, the meeting was over. Edward and Marian rose from their seats to leave, relieved that there would not be the bloodshed they had feared. Marian's brave words had served their purpose.

But less happy was Guy of Gisborne. He approached the Sheriff. 'My lord. I still believe – action rather than words… If I had the resources I could deal with him, I could hunt him down…'

The Sheriff considered him for a moment. After all, he had no desire to see Robin go entirely free, and it wouldn't clash with his other plans. Why not let Gisborne have a shot at bringing down the man who was rapidly becoming a rather painful thorn in his side? 'Very well,' he said. 'Then do.'

Gisborne left the room happy.

CHAPTER THREE

It was the sort of funeral usually reserved for the most important, the most influential, and the wealthiest. Not for a humble bailiff. But the Sheriff was putting on a show. Joderic, he was demonstrating with the banners and the heralds and the crowds of noble mourners, was the sort of person that mattered. The sort of person that counted for something in an unjust world. The sort of person that there could be no justification at all for killing.

The crowd in the castle courtyard listened to the Sheriff weaving his spell. No one who listened could be in any doubt of the evil that had been done when Joderic was cut down. The man who committed the deed could not be counted as anyone's friend; he was no champion of the poor but a ruthless criminal.

Several of these alleged ruthless criminals were hidden nearby, listening to the words condemning them. Much was getting increasingly indignant as the Sheriff's speech continued.

'Joderic was unique. Kind, compassionate, learned. The murder of Joderic was the murder of knowledge, the murder of charity, the murder of innocence. He taught so many to read, opened our minds, made us better than we were. And all that was gone in a moment, gone with one arrow from the bow of Robin Hood…'

Much couldn't contain himself any longer. 'He is saying you killed Joderic!' he told Robin, furious at the injustice.

But Robin didn't seem surprised. 'Of course he is.'

'He's making us look like criminals!'

Roy, crouched down beside Much, shrugged his shoulders. 'You know, I think we *are* criminals. What, are we something else now?' he asked as Much looked even more indignant.

Then Much noticed what Robin was doing, and his expression changed from indignation to worry. Because Robin had pulled an arrow from his quiver and was fitting it to his bow. What trouble would they be in for now?

Allan A Dale had noticed too. 'Hang on, hang on, that's a bit bold, isn't it?'

But Robin just smiled at his companions as he raised the bow and took careful aim. 'It's not bold, it's *pointless*…'

Also listening to the Sheriff's speech, and with just as much disbelief as Robin and his men, were Marian and Edward. Both were here to show their respect for the man who had died – the man they knew the Sheriff had cared nothing for, despite his fine words.

'We'll leave as soon as Joderic's buried,' Edwards said quietly to his daughter. 'We can say you were too upset.'

'I *am* too upset,' Marian pointed out.

And it looked like she wasn't the only one. Near them, standing apart from the crowd, was a wiry, intense-looking man, who looked as though he was about to break down at any moment. Marian recognised Joe Lacey, who had once been one of the castle archers, and hurried over to him. She knew he was still grieving the death of his wife – he was in no state to have resumed his duties for the Sheriff.

'Joe, what are you doing here?' she asked, concerned. 'You cannot work.'

Lacey seemed to summon up his reply from a long distance. 'They've made everyone come back in. Called me out of retirement.'

'I will speak to the Sheriff,' Marian told him. 'I'll get you off your duties.'

But Lacey shook his head tiredly. 'Work helps. I still reach out for her in the night. I know it's daft.'

Marian shook her head compassionately. 'It's not daft. When this is over you're coming home with us.'

Lacey barely seemed to take in her words. He was looking instead at the crowd, peasants and nobles alike crowding around Joderic's coffin. 'Where were all this lot when we put my Ruth in the ground?'

Marian couldn't answer him. None of this was fair. None of this was right. She put out a hand to console him as the Sheriff's insincere words continued.

'This reminds us all of the stark choice we face. Between stability, order and authority... and the random, chaotic cruelty of Robin Hood and outlaws like him. We will not be cowed. We stand strong. We hunt these people down. And when we catch Robin Hood – make no mistake – this cowardly crime will be punished.'

And, as the nobles applauded the speech, eager to ingratiate themselves with the Sheriff without thought for the solemn dignity of the occasion they were supposed to be observing, something hit Marian on the bottom.

She moved away from Joe Lacey, turning to see what had stung her. There on the ground behind her was an arrow. A *pointless* arrow, its tip blunted. And she knew exactly who the arrow belonged to...

It took Marian a few moments to locate Robin, hidden on the other side of a portcullis. While a priest began the funeral rites, and the rest of the outlaws kept a careful lookout for the Sheriff and his men, she went to join him, alone, the arrow clutched angrily in one hand.

'You are fetching in mourning,' Robin told her, grinning, but she was in no mood for glib compliments.

'*Never* shoot me again,' she informed him forcefully, thrusting the arrow back at him. 'Do you understand?'

Robin inclined his head in apology, but she

could tell he didn't really mean it, that he regretted nothing. There was a definite smirk lurking just on the edges of his apparently contrite expression.

'What do you want?' she asked impatiently.

Robin gestured towards the courtyard, where the priest was still intoning solemn Latin phrases. 'This is all in my honour, isn't it?'

'You really do think everything is about you, don't you?' Marian said.

He shrugged, not bothered by the sting in her words. 'Only when it *is* about me.'

Marian looked over at the funeral. The Sheriff still stood there overseeing the proceedings, looking concerned. Oh, she might not agree with what Robin was doing, not by a long way, but she understood why he was doing it. 'You've given him a stick to beat you with. You killed an innocent clerk. So here he is, making the most of it.'

There was silence for a moment. She turned back to Robin, who was staring at her intently. She met his gaze: there was no hint of a smirk there now. 'I did not do it,' he said.

And, looking into his eyes, she could not help but believe him. Really, she'd known it all along. 'I'm sure,' she said.

But his next words were less welcome. 'It was this so-called non-violent Nightwatchman,' Robin told her.

She shook her head. 'No.'

'I saw him,' Robin insisted. 'I was there.'

Marian shook her head again, annoyed. 'It was *not* the Nightwatchman.'

'How do you know?' he asked.

'I know.'

But Robin, irritating, stubborn Robin, would not be convinced. 'Then why did he run? He is guilty.'

She frowned, angry that he wouldn't listen to her. 'You ran from Joderic – does that mean you're guilty?'

He opened his mouth to answer, but a tolling bell cut across their conversation. Funeral chimes. It was time to leave: she would be missed.

'I should go.' She took a step forward.

But Robin was reluctant to stand aside for her. He put out a pleading hand. 'You must help me.'

'I am helping you,' Marian insisted. 'I'm telling you – it is not the Nightwatchman.'

Robin still wouldn't let her go. 'Whoever it is, I'll find him. And I can look everywhere apart from one place – I need you to look in the castle.'

'I need you to not tell me what to do,' Marian replied stiffly.

But Robin was still fixing her with that urgent, soulful gaze. 'Please. I must clear my name.'

Marian broke eye contact and moved past him. But as his words sank in she turned back. 'What about catching a killer? Isn't that more important than your name?'

He shrugged hopelessly. 'If people do not trust me, then what good can I do?'

And as Marian finally made her way back to her father, she reflected that, much as it pained her to admit it, Robin had a very good point.

CHAPTER FOUR

If Robin had not killed Joderic, and the Nightwatchman had not killed him, then somewhere in Nottingham a secret killer lurked. And as one of the few people who realised this, Marian knew she had to help track him down. For justice – and for Robin. So the next day, she attempted to put Robin's plan into action. She would go to Nottingham Castle, find a way of getting access to its ins and outs, its many chambers and passageways, and she would search for the assassin.

She tried to hide her disquiet as she arrived in the castle grounds to find a hunting expedition taking shape. These were Gisborne's troops, out to catch Robin! Gisborne himself was moving through the crowd of soldiers and hunters, happily admiring a horse here, a viciously barking hunting dog there. Looking less happy was De Fourtnoy, also watching the troops and the fearsome attack dogs, but from a greater distance. Marian heard Gisborne smugly call out to him. 'Tell me, is Master at Arms just a ceremonial position now? Because problems like Hood demand real solutions.' He gestured at the milling soldiers, and said condescendingly, 'Town criers?' And with a smirk, he swept past the resentful Master at Arms, towards where Marian stood.

She stepped forward to greet him. 'Sir Guy.'

'Marian.'

'All these dogs for one man?' she said, concealing her true feelings beneath a cool gaze.

Gisborne nodded proudly. 'It was my idea. The Master at Arms…' he shot a disparagingly look back to where De Fourtnoy still stood, 'would have us do nothing.'

'You are in competition?' she asked innocently.

Marian smiled inside to see the impact her simple question had made. Gisborne, desperate to be regarded as superior to the other man, could not possibly admit that was the case. 'No,' he replied, a little too hastily. He hurried to clarify the position. 'He is a little man, promoted too far. One of my troops would make a far better Master at Arms.'

'And get you a share of the budget,' Marian said, before she could stop herself. She cursed inside, seeing Gisborne's eyebrows raised at this insight.

It could be dangerous if he realised that she thought about these things; worse if he realised she understood a great deal more about the situation than a mere woman was supposed to. She hurried to cover herself. 'I'm guessing. I try to understand these things, but… Politics.' She smiled, a girl out of her depth. 'Even when my father was Sheriff, I could not grasp the intricacies.' Gisborne seemed to accept this. Well, she thought bitterly, it was what he wanted to believe. She hastened to change the subject. 'My father sent me here, by the way. He thinks it's safer – with a killer on the loose – and…'

Gisborne interrupted. 'You say " a killer"? You do not think it is Hood?'

This was not a debate Marian thought it a good idea to get into just now. She merely shrugged. 'Whoever it is, my father thought I should stay in the castle.'

'That is not permitted,' Gisborne informed her.

Marian allowed herself to look disappointed. One good thing about being a 'mere woman', was that it made it so easy to manipulate mere men.

'I'll speak to the Sheriff,' Gisborne said. He moved off towards the men, but Marian could tell his air of command was being assumed as much for her benefit as for theirs. 'I want a line sweeping south through the forest. Break every bush. Look up into every tree. Drop the hounds into every hollow. He will run.'

And Marian, watching the determined faces of the hunters and the eagerness of the barking dogs, was worried that, this time, Gisborne might be right.

Robin and his men had no idea of what was coming for them – until they heard the dogs. Big, fierce Little John was the first to catch the sound on the wind and alerted the others. Robin, Much, Roy and Allan froze, trying to detect the barking for themselves, hoping John was mistaken. But Will Scarlett's arrival left them with no hope at all. He staggered into the camp, breathless and gasping, panic in his eyes.

'The King's Guild of Hunters and Foresters – coming for us! Dogs!'

Much looked as if he was about to be sick. 'Oh no. Surely…'

But Robin gave him no time to finish his sentence. He was on his feet and gesturing for the

39

others to do the same. 'Pairs,' he snapped, waving at Little John and Roy, Allan and Will. 'Meet where we stored the provisions. Go.' They didn't protest but instantly split into the twos he'd indicated and ran off into the forest in different directions. Robin swiftly put out their fire before speeding off in a third direction with Much at his side, pausing only to pick up a dead rabbit which had been lying on the ground ready for a later meal.

'This is bad, isn't it?' Much gasped as they fled. 'Be honest with me.'

But while Much's fears were of the hunters and the dogs catching up with them, Robin's concerns were elsewhere. 'Yes, it's bad,' he agreed. 'While this goes on we can't find the killer.'

Much couldn't be distracted from the thought of their potential fate. 'At least he uses the bow,' he said. 'A surprise arrow is quick. But we are hunted by dogs...' The howls of the hounds reached them across the treetops. 'I have never liked dogs,' Much concluded, as they plunged into the thick undergrowth.

The barks of the dogs were getting louder and Much's panic was getting greater. 'They have caught our scent!' he sobbed. But Robin put a finger to his lips, then leant down and dragged the dead rabbit along the ground. As the dogs neared, he dropped it and darted off into cover, Much still stumbling by his side. They crouched in the bushes, not daring to move, as the horses approached. Sir Guy of Gisborne was heading the riders, and his face glowed at the purposeful yelping and barking of the dogs – he clearly believed his quarry was as good as caught. But even the terrified Much felt like laughing as he watched Gisborne's face fall a moment later – when the dogs emerged from the bushes dragging nothing but a dead rabbit. Furious, he gave the sign to move on. As the hunt rode off, Robin and Much made their way back on to the path, and their expressions – unlike Gisborne's – were triumphant.

CHAPTER FIVE

The dogs were still barking many hours later; the Sheriff could hear them from his bedchamber. Although he was dressed in his nightshirt he was not resting but working, ploughing his way through the many papers on his desk. He'd called for wine and now it arrived, carried by a timid servant boy. Despite his earlier protestations of admiration for Joderic and concern for the people, the Sheriff neither knew nor cared that this boy was Matthew, son of Kate and Owen who had watched his bailiff die.

Matthew nervously poured a goblet of wine for the Sheriff and placed it and the carafe at his master's elbow. He turned to go, but the Sheriff stopped him. 'Wait, new boy. Am I left-handed?'

The terrified Matthew turned back fearfully.

'A clue: no.'

Now Matthew realised his mistake. He hurried forward and moved the carafe and still untouched goblet to the other side of the desk, within reach of the Sheriff's right hand. The Sheriff said nothing, and, praying he'd done the right thing this time, the boy once more went to leave.

But the Sheriff hadn't finished with him. Not even looking up from his work, he said: 'Stand on one leg.'

Halfway to the door, Matthew froze, not understanding.

'Right leg. One hour. Then you might remember.'

Confused and scared, Matthew obeyed the Sheriff's command. Now the Sheriff finally looked at him, enjoying the boy's bewilderment. He stood up, walking past Matthew to the window and looked out into the gloom. A distant howl reached them on the wind.

Still staring outside, the Sheriff said, 'What do you think of your new job, new boy? Could be worse. You could be running through the forest hunted by dogs.'

He turned from the window, back to Matthew, although he clearly did not expect the boy to answer.

And Matthew didn't answer; would never answer again, as an arrow flew through the window and hit him in the chest. He collapsed to the floor, one leg buckled under him in cruel parody of the position he'd been forced to assume.

The Sheriff threw himself down, yelling for the guards, his spilled wine mingling with the growing pool of blood from the dying boy. But the Sheriff didn't spare him a glance: he was too concerned with examining his own arm, caught in passing by the speeding arrow.

Guards rushed in and the Sheriff shouted at them to raise the alarm. As they ran off to do so, De Fourtnoy pushed his way into the room.

'I'm dying,' croaked the tiny, weak voice of Matthew from the floor, still bewildered, still scared, but now hurting too; trying to make sense of what was happening to him.

But De Fourtnoy ignored him just as the Sheriff had.

'In my own *room*? *My own room*?' the Sheriff was raging. He pulled himself to his feet, taking care to stay well clear of the window. 'Where are the men?' he demanded of De Fourtnoy.

'Gisborne has taken them to hunt Hood with the dogs,' the Master at Arms informed him, struggling to hide his pleasure that his rival would incur the

Sheriff's wrath.

'Gisborne is a fool.'

'Hood clearly has evaded him,' De Fourtnoy pointed out, gesturing at the arrow protruding from Matthew's chest, but the Sheriff shook his head.

'This is not Robin Hood. He doesn't miss.' He stood for a second, marshalling his thoughts. 'Lock down the castle. Tell Gisborne to scrap his dogs. Find the killer.' The Sheriff finally looked down at the boy at his feet, finally seemed to notice that someone else had been involved in the attack. 'And get this one out of here.' Finally acknowledging that Matthew was there. Although in his eyes the boy wasn't Matthew. He was just a dead body in the Sheriff's way.

De Fourtnoy nodded and was about to leave the room when the Sheriff stopped him. 'Tell Gisborne to double the dogs.'

The Master at Arms was bewildered. 'But my lord, I thought you said... It cannot be him.'

The Sheriff interrupted. 'Two words: mud sticks. Hood's already been blamed for one death, let's blame him for two.'

A smile spread across De Fourtnoy's face,

appreciating the cunning of the Sheriff's plan.

'Let Gisborne have his hunt. You, meanwhile…'
De Fourtnoy bowed his head in acquiescence, 'will
find out who did this.'

The Master at Arms, convinced that he was
favoured over Gisborne, happily agreed.

Sir Guy of Gisborne was annoyed that he had
to take a break from leading the hunt personally,
but pleased that the Sheriff had sent him to be
his representative at the boy Matthew's funeral. It
showed, he was convinced, that he was favoured over
others – such as that jumped-up De Fourtnoy.

But while Gisborne viewed the occasion solely
as a step to his own advancement, the villagers
of Nettlestone could barely contain their grief.
They had not yet recovered from the death of
Joderic, and now, a mere two days later, had to
mourn a tragedy much closer to home. They just
acknowledged the presence of Gisborne, leading
Matthew's pathetic coffin home, as a gesture of
respect from the Sheriff – or so they thought – but
took little notice of him beyond that.

Until he began to speak.

The funeral was underway. Owen stood by the

coffin, tears streaming down his face. So wrapped up was he in his own sorrow that he did not even have a shred of comfort to spare for his wife; Kate was being supported by Joe Lacey — there with the rest of the castle archers — who himself understood grief only too well.

And it was then that Gisborne spoke.

'We pray for Matthew's soul as he journeys to a better place. Watch over us, Matthew, and be proud.' He raised his voice. 'We will bring Robin Hood to justice. You have my word.'

And one by one the mourners took in those words. It was Robin Hood. It was Robin Hood who did this, who took away one of their own.

Robin Hood would pay.

And Gisborne realised that he was still, at that very minute, leading the hunt. But this hunt needed no dogs.

Back in the castle, the Sheriff — accompanied by a unit of guards for protection — returned to his bedchamber. Inside, he found two workmen busy boarding up the windows. Furious, he ordered them to get out, and then turned to De Fourtnoy, who had joined him. 'What is this?'

'A precaution,' De Fourtnoy explained. 'We must take every precaution.'

But the Sheriff – who De Fourtnoy knew would be the first to cast blame were he left unprotected – huffed angrily at this. 'Precautions? I'm hiding in my own castle. I cannot move in my own castle!'

The Master at Arms hastened to reassure him. 'We are leaving no stone unturned, my lord. He will be found.'

'No stone unturned, la de dah… just get on with it.'

De Fourtnoy, realising that being favoured by the Sheriff was not without its disadvantages, bowed and left the room. As he reached the corridor, the Sheriff called after him. 'How's Gisborne doing with Locksley?'

The Master at Arms smiled. However difficult the Sheriff was to deal with, at least he was not in Robin Hood's shoes… 'More dogs have been brought in,' he replied. 'But the outlaw is still on the run.'

'Have you had it put about that he killed twice?'

'Yes, my lord,' De Fourtnoy assured him, stepping back into the room. He waited a moment to see if he was once again dismissed, but the Sheriff seemed to be in thought. Finally he spoke.

'Do you think two deaths is enough?'

De Fourtnoy opened his mouth to answer, but nothing came out. He wasn't sure what the Sheriff meant, and dared not say the wrong thing. Luckily for him the Sheriff hadn't finished.

'To get them really to turn against him? The rabble? I'm not sure. What do you think? I think maybe a few more deaths. Would be interesting. Pretty deaths – not just boys.'

And then De Fourtnoy knew exactly what the Sheriff meant, and exactly what was required of him.

CHAPTER SIX

Gisborne had honoured his promise to Marian and she was now established in the castle — although Matthew's death gave lie to the idea that she would want to be there for safety. So far, her investigations had not progressed to any great extent, but she was determined and persistent — if the murderer was here to discover, then she would discover him.

She was just trying to determine her next move when she heard a scream. It came from the direction of the courtyard, and she ran out towards it. Lying on the ground was a young maid, an arrow in her back. Others were approaching, a couple pointing up towards the tower. That must be where the arrow had come from. Marian looked up — a movement, the swiftest glance of a sleeve sweeping by a window. She hesitated, then continued towards the crowd that was rapidly growing around the poor maid's body.

Suddenly De Fourtnoy appeared at her side, his

bow clutched tightly in his hand. 'Marian? Come away, if you please.'

Marian turned to him. 'Robert. I thought you had locked down the castle. How could this happen?'

De Fourtnoy didn't answer, but continued insistently, 'Return to your room, please. It is not safe.'

Marian could hardly argue with that – and to do so might seem suspicious. She nodded her head and turned to go. But as De Fourtnoy moved off in the other direction, towards the dead maid, she surreptitiously stared at his sleeve. Was it – could it possibly be – the same one she had glimpsed in the tower?

Was De Fourtnoy the mystery murderer?

Over the course of the day, the castle's inhabitants began to think it would be safer to be fighting the Saracens with King Richard than going about their daily business at home. Mere hours after the maid had been slaughtered, a stable boy was killed by an arrow while mending a saddle. A short time after that, a footman was struck down as he carried food from the kitchens.

Marian was frustrated – as well as angry and unhappy. She had never been on the scene of the crime as quickly again, and had no chance to spy once again that telltale sleeve – or perhaps some greater clue. She was also unable to keep De Fourtnoy in view – his duties led him to places where her presence would create suspicion, and she had to be careful not to appear too reckless, as everyone seemed so concerned about her safety, the reason she had used for staying at the castle in the first place.

Still, she had to keep trying. Because despite what the castle servants were saying all around her, she knew full well that the culprit was not Robin.

And she shivered as she thought of what Robin might be going through at that moment...

Allan and Will staggered towards a clearing – the rendezvous point.

'This is not what I imagined when I joined up,' Allan was saying, looking back nervously over his shoulder. They had evaded the dogs for now – but both were only too aware that the hunt was still out there.

'What did you imagine?' Will asked.

'Don't know. But this is not it.'

Allan might have said more – but at that moment they entered the clearing, and both were struck dumb in horror.

There were Robin and Much, Little John and Roy – and the remains of every scrap the outlaws owned. Food and weapons alike were little more than charred remains, a few wisps of smoke still curling up teasingly from the pile. Their provisions had been found, dug up – and utterly destroyed. Now they had nothing.

'That was our store,' Much told the newcomers, needlessly. 'That was our food.'

They all stared at the ashes. It almost hurt more than the thought of the relentless dogs, imagining the smile on Gisborne's face as he ordered their few pathetic resources burned. They would have to gather more if they wanted to survive – if they even managed to survive the next few hours. A sudden volley of barking brought them out of their frozen reverie – the dogs were getting near.

As one, the exhausted outlaws took to their heels again.

Eventually, the sound of the dogs faded in the distance, and they allowed themselves a few moments respite, sinking down to the forest floor. Will Scarlett alone stumbled on, with Much watching after him in hope.

'Do you think Will will bring water?' he asked. He thought a little more. 'Some bread would not go amiss either. Perhaps a piece of cheese. Or both.'

Roy looked at him incredulously. 'Cheese? We're going to get captured, tortured and hanged – and he wants cheese?'

Robin, who knew Much's stomach of old, grinned at this, but Much himself was indignant. 'I must say –' he began, but Roy cut him off.

'Shut up, cheese boy.'

They sat in silence for a few minutes, and despite Roy's words, more than one outlaw was now thinking longingly of Much's bread and cheese, whatever threats they had hanging over them.

But then the threats were brought back into sharp focus as the howling of the dogs reached them once more. Groaning, the five men pulled themselves to their feet.

'Don't they ever give up?' Roy muttered, but they all knew the answer to that.

Much turned, trying to summon up the energy

to run – and noticed that instead of joining the rest of them, Robin had stayed exactly where he was – and had pulled his bow off his shoulder.

The howling was getting louder.

'Master – the dogs,' said Much urgently. 'We cannot stay!'

Robin did not look at him; he was staring into the distance as he nocked an arrow. Much recognised that expression: he had seen it during battles when there had been a choice of fight or flight. Robin had always preferred to stand up to his enemies; never put safety first when there was work to do.

It was a way of life that had left poor Much in an almost permanent state of terror.

Robin looked grim. 'I must do *something*. We are running away when we should be in pursuit.' Much groaned inwardly. 'The Nightwatchman is out there, free.'

Yes, but he doesn't have a pack of deadly dogs after him, Much thought. Surely – *surely* – even Robin could not intend to take on hounds, huntsmen, Gisborne – all with a handful of arrows and a few exhausted men?

The howling got louder still. All thoughts of

food vanished from Much's mind, crowded out by everything else Roy had mentioned – the capture, the torture, the hanging. If the dogs did not rip them to pieces first.

And then – oh blessed relief! – Robin lowered his bow and turned around. 'We head east. Where we last saw the Nightwatchman.'